Barkus

BOOK 1

BY PATRICIA MACLACHLAN · ILLUSTRATED BY MARC BOUTAVANT

chronicle books · san francisco

In memory of my neighbor, Barkus,
a sweet dog thief who "borrowed" the toys of my dogs—
His life was full.
So was his toy basket. —P. M.

Text © 2017 by Patricia MacLachlan.
Illustrations © 2017 by Marc Boutavant.

Library of Congress Cataloging-in-Publication Data:

Names: MacLachlan, Patricia, author. | Boutavant, Marc, illustrator.
Title: Barkus / by Patricia MacLachlan ; illustrated by Marc Boutavant.
Description: San Francisco : Chronicle Books, [2017] | Summary: Barkus is a
large and very smart dog who comes to live with seven-year-old Nicky, when
Nicky's Uncle Everton goes traveling—and soon he is a family and school favorite.
Identifiers: LCCN 2016006995 | ISBN 9781452111827 (alk. paper)
Subjects: LCSH: Dogs—Juvenile fiction. | CYAC: Dogs—Fiction.
Classification: LCC PZ7.M2225 Bar 2017 | DDC [E]—dc23 LC record available at http://lccn.loc.gov/2016006995

Manufactured in China.

Design by Sara Gillingham Studio.
Typeset in Harriet and Lunchbox.

10 9 8 7 6 5 4 3 2 1

Chronicle Books LLC
680 Second Street,
San Francisco, California 94107
Chronicle Books—we see things differently. Become part of our community at www.chroniclekids.com.

CONTENTS

BARKUS

On a windy day, my favorite uncle, Uncle Everton, knocked on our door. He wore a long plaid overcoat and black wool cap.

"I've brought a present!" he called.

"Who is the present for?" I asked.

"You, Nicky!" roared Uncle Everton happily.

Uncle Everton held a leash. At one end was Uncle Everton. At the other end was . . .

. . . a very big brown dog!

"Oh my," said my mother.

"He's big," said my father.

"His name is Barkus," said Uncle Everton. "I'll be traveling around the world. Barkus does not like to travel. He would rather stay with you."

I patted Barkus.

"Barkus is very smart," Uncle Everton said. "Smartest dog in the whole world."

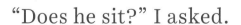

"Does he sit?" I asked.

Barkus sat on my foot.

"He likes you already!" said Uncle Everton.

"Does he do tricks?" I asked.

"Yes," said Uncle Everton. "Many tricks.
Jump, Barkus."

Barkus jumped.
"Whirl around,"
said Uncle Everton.

Barkus whirled and whirled.

"Does he get along with people?" asked my mother.

"Yes," said Uncle Everton.

"Does he bark?" asked my father.

"Only when he wants to," said Uncle Everton.

"Is there anything Barkus doesn't do?" I asked.

"Yes," said Uncle Everton. "Barkus doesn't bite."

"Then I'll keep him!" I said. "Thank you."

"You're welcome," said Uncle Everton.

And that is how Barkus became my dog!

BARKUS
SNEAKS

It was Monday morning.

I put on my sweater and coat and boots.

Barkus watched me.

I put on my gloves.

Barkus watched me.

"Goodbye, Barkus. I'll see you after school."

I patted him on the head.

I went out the door.

When I looked back Barkus was watching through the window.

I walked down Willow Street. There were leaves on the sidewalk and my boots made a crunching sound in the leaves. Soon I heard another sound.

I turned.

But there were only green pine trees there.

I began walking again.

I heard the sound again.

I turned.

Nothing.

When I got to school I opened the door.

Barkus
rushed
in!

Mrs. Gregolian, my teacher, smiled.

"Who is this, Nicky?" she asked.

"My new dog, Barkus," I said. "He followed me to school. He is a sneak."

"Is he friendly?" asked Mrs. Gregolian.

"Yes," I said. "And he doesn't bite."

"That's very good," said Mrs. Gregolian. "Can he sit quietly?"

"Yes," I said. "Sit, Barkus."

Barkus sat next to my desk.

He helped me paint a picture.

He read a book with me.

When Mrs. Gregolian wrote the letters

D O G on the blackboard, Barkus barked.

"I think Barkus knows his letters!" Mrs. Gregolian said. "Maybe he will help us all learn to read."

"Yes!" said the children.

And that is how Barkus became our class dog.

A BARK
IN THE DARK

A small package came in the mail. It was from Uncle Everton. It was three dog cookies with a red ribbon tied around them. And there was a note:

Dear BARKUS,
Happy Birthday!

"It's your birthday!" I said to Barkus.

But Barkus was not paying attention. He was chewing on a cookie.

"Maybe you can have a birthday party at school tomorrow," I said.

But the next day something happened.

Snow. Lots of snow!

"No school today, Barkus," my mother said.

Barkus and I went outside to play in the snow.

We ran.

We jumped.

We ate snow.

"We'll have a quiet little party for him after dinner," said my mother.

"I don't think Barkus wants a quiet party," I said. "I think he wants a noisy party."

After dinner we had a quiet birthday party for Barkus.

He got a ball.

He got a tug toy.

Barkus rolled the ball.

Barkus chewed the tug toy.

But he looked sad.

He stood in the window and looked out into the darkness. He looked out for a long time.

"What's wrong, Barkus?" I asked. "Why are you sad?"

And then we heard it.

A bark in the dark!

Then two more barks!

Bark! Bark!

When I opened the door there were three
dogs.

His friends had come to his party!

Barkus and his friends ran and jumped.

They ate dog cookies.

They whirled and twirled and swirled.

They ate dog cookies.

They yipped and pounced and bounced off the sofa!

And ate dog cookies.

Barkus was happy.

And that is how Barkus got . . .

. . . a very

noisy party!

BARKUS FINDS
A BABY

Spring had come and it was vacation.

I was bored.

Barkus was bored.

"Barkus needs something new and exciting,"
I said.

"I don't think Barkus needs something new
and exciting," said my father.

But he was wrong.

One day, we saw Barkus coming down the
street with something in his mouth. He was
holding it very carefully.

Barkus walked up the sidewalk and put it
down on the porch.

It meowed.

"It's a kitten!" I said.

"It certainly is," said my mother.

The kitten meowed again.

My father brought a small saucer of water.

The kitten lapped it up.

"I told you Barkus wanted something new and exciting," I said.

"You did," said my father. "But this kitten probably belongs to someone. We'd better find out."

My mother called the neighbors. My father put up signs asking if anyone was missing a kitten.

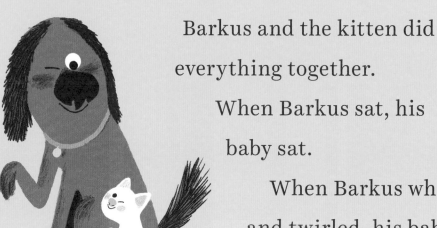

Barkus and the kitten did
everything together.

When Barkus sat, his
baby sat.

When Barkus whirled
and twirled, his baby
whirled and twirled.

When Barkus
jumped up on the
couch where he wasn't
supposed to be, his baby
jumped up on the couch
where *she* wasn't
supposed to be.

At night Barkus and his baby curled up together at the foot of my bed.

Barkus and his baby were very happy.

"I hope no one calls," I said.

"The kitten is Barkus's baby."

Barkus wagged his tail.

My mother smiled.

"I hope no one calls, too," she whispered to me.

And then one day a woman came to the house.

"Did you find a kitten?" she asked.

She patted Barkus, and then she saw his baby hiding under him.

"Oh, there she is," she said.

"This is my dog, Barkus. He has adopted your kitten," I said. "She is his new baby."

The woman smiled.

"Well, I'm glad to see she has a good home. I have four more kittens to find homes for," she said.

"*Her* home is here," I said.

"I think you're right," the woman said. "And does the baby have a name?"

"No," I said. "No name."

What about Tessie?

asked my mother.

Barkus was quiet.

What about Rascal?

asked my father.

Barkus was quiet.

What about Miss Pudge?

asked the woman.

Barkus yawned.

"I guess we'll just have to call her Baby,"
I said.

Barkus sat up and barked!

"Baby!" I said. "That's the name Barkus wants!"

Barkus barked again!

Baby sat up and meowed.

And that was how Baby came to have a name.

THE STORY

My father put up a tent
in the backyard.

"What do you do in a tent?" I asked.

"You eat snacks. You tell stories. And you sleep," said my father.

"Maybe I'll be afraid of the dark," I said.

"You'll have a flashlight," said my father. "You will not be afraid of the dark."

I packed snacks and sandwiches for me.

I packed snacks for Barkus and Baby.

I packed a carton of juice for me.

I put out a bowl of water for Barkus and Baby.

I put two sleeping bags inside the tent.

One for Barkus and Baby.

One for me.

Soon it was
nighttime.
I crawled into
the tent.

Barkus and Baby crawled into the tent.

It was dark inside.

I turned on my flashlight.

"First let's have snacks," I said.

Barkus and Baby were happy to eat snacks.

I drank my juice.

Barkus and Baby drank water.

"Now I will tell you the story of a boy named Hansel and a girl named Gretel who meet a witch," I began.

Barkus whined.

"Not that story?" I said. "Then I'll tell a story about a boy who climbs a giant beanstalk. Once there was a boy named Jack."

Barkus whined.

"Not that story, either?"

I yawned.

"I can only think of one more story to tell," I said.

"Once upon a time there was a favorite uncle named Uncle Everton. He brought me a present! And that present was Barkus!"

Barkus sat up and listened. Baby sat up and listened.

"Barkus went to school and the children loved him. The teacher, Mrs. Gregolian,

42

loved Barkus, too, and she and Barkus helped us learn how to read. Once Barkus had a very noisy birthday party with his dog friends. And then Barkus found something new and exciting! And that new and exciting thing was Baby!"

Barkus and Baby were very quiet. They lay down on their sleeping bag.

"Now Barkus and Baby live with us. And we are a very, very happy family."

I shined the flashlight on Barkus and Baby. They were asleep.

"The End," I whispered. I turned off the flashlight.

And I was not afraid of the dark.